DANBI
Leads the School Parade

by

Anna Kim

VIKING

To all the new kids on the block and those who have the power to make them feel welcome.

With all my thanks to Steve Malk, who made this book possible.

———•———

VIKING

An imprint of Penguin Random House LLC

New York

First published in the United States of America by Viking, an imprint of Penguin Random House LLC, 2020

LIBRARY OF CONGRESS CATALOGING-IN-PUBLICATION DATA IS AVAILABLE.

ISBN 9780451478894

1   3   5   7   9   10   8   6   4   2

Manufactured in China   Set in LTC Kennerley Pro   Design by Nancy Brennan

On the first day of my new school in America,
my heart beat: *Boom. Boom.*

Mama held me and whispered,
"Listen to your teacher and eat your lunch."
I said, "Don't worry, Mama, I'll be good today!"
and I walked through the big red door.

Boom. Boom.

Everyone stared.

But I didn't blink.

The teacher handed me a marker,
but I wasn't sure why. *Boom. Boom.*

So I wrote my name, "Danbi," in perfect straight lines.

It means "sweet rain" in Korean.
But no one knew that here.

When the music started,
I tried dances I'd never seen,

and games I didn't know.

I tried,

and tried,

and tried again.

But no one
played with me.

Clap. Clap.
The teacher said something,
and everyone pulled out their
lunches.

That, I knew how to do!

Yams in honey, crystal dumplings,
sweet-and-sour mini skewers,
rainbow drops, and half-moon rice
cakes dipped in sweet sesame!
All my favorites!

"Wow!" everyone cried.

The girl with pigtails looked
and looked, so I gave her
a rainbow drop.

Uh-oh!
This wasn't working!

So I showed her how it's done....

Everyone wanted to try it, too.
Click-clack. Click-clack.

That gave me an idea!

TING!

I tapped my lunch box.

ding!

She tapped her juice box.

And then . . .

it got a little wild.

BOOM BOOM
TAP TAP!

Let's have a parade!

We took over the
classroom . . .

and the playground.

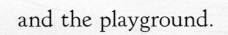

I had a feeling
I might like it here.

At the end of the
day, I pointed to
my nose and
said, "Danbi."

She put her
hand on her
chest and said,
"I'm Nelly."

Nelly showed me how to write my name in big round letters.

And together, we wrote our
names on our cubbies.

That night, I told Mama,
"I made a new friend!
We'll play again tomorrow!"

She smiled her big smile.

On the fog of the window,
I wrote my name.

Soft and round,
with a dot just above
one straight line.

AUTHOR'S NOTE

I will never forget my first day of school in America. I remember standing in front of the whole class, everyone staring at me, not understanding a word from the teacher. I eventually learned English and grew up to embrace my bicultural identity, but the shock of that first day and the feeling of being an outsider stayed with me. And so, when my nieces were born, I looked for fun picture books featuring heroic characters with whom they could identify. If those characters existed, I didn't find them, and that is what inspired me to create Danbi.

There's a postscript to my first day at school. A few months later, my classmate Mia and I became friends. She was kind and gentle, and I remember her smile to this day. She may not have known it at the time, but her friendship was the first step in my journey to feeling at home in America. My hope is that, in reading this story, children will see a bit of themselves in Danbi and want her as a friend. It is my deep belief that bridging our differences happens one human being at a time and that, once we've connected as friends, we can begin to celebrate our differences.

This book wouldn't exist without the faith and guidance of Steve Malk at Writers House and Ken Wright, Tamar Brazis, and Nancy Brennan at Viking Books. I'm also immensely grateful to my parents for the sacrifices they made in bringing my brothers and me to America; to my nieces Audrey and Christie for introducing me to the wonderful world of picture books; and to my partner Hugues Farges for helping shape Danbi and her story.